THIS CANDLEWICK BOOK BELONGS TO:

_____

_____

_____

First paperback edition 2009

Library of Congress Cataloging-in-Publication Data is available.
Library of Congress Catalog Card Number 2006051839

ISBN 978-0-7636-2499-6 (hardcover)
ISBN 978-0-7636-4284-6 (paperback)

17 18 CCP 25 24

Printed in Shenzhen, Guangdong, China

This book was typeset in Univers.
The illustrations were done in watercolor, pencil,
and ink and were assembled digitally.

Candlewick Press
99 Dover Street
Somerville, Massachusetts 02144

visit us at www.candlewick.com

To the Condon family and to Kara,
for living life so generously

M. B.

For Kevin, who has always been a wonderful friend
and a horrible Scrabble player

N. Z. J.

Those Shoes

Maribeth Boelts
illustrated by Noah Z. Jones

CANDLEWICK PRESS

I have dreams about those shoes.
Black high-tops. Two white stripes.

"Grandma, I want them."

"There's no room for 'want' around here—just 'need,'"
Grandma says. "And what you *need* are new boots for winter."

Brandon T. comes to school in those shoes. He says he's the fastest runner now, not me. I was always the fastest before those shoes came along.

Nate comes to school in those shoes. Antonio and I count how many times Nate goes to the bathroom—seven times in one day, just so he can walk up and down the hall real slow.

Next, Allen Jacoby and Terrence each get a pair.

Then one day, in the middle of kickball, one of my shoes comes apart.

"Looks like you could use a new pair, Jeremy," Mr. Alfrey, the guidance counselor, says. He brings out a box of shoes and other stuff he has for kids who need things. He helps me find the only shoes that are my size—Velcro—like the ones my little cousin Marshall wears. They have an animal on them from a cartoon I don't think any kid ever watched.

When I come back to the classroom, Allen Jacoby takes
one look at my Mr. Alfrey shoes and laughs, and so do
Terrence, Brandon T., and everyone else. The only kid not
laughing is Antonio Parker.

At home, Grandma says, "How kind of Mr. Alfrey." I nod
and turn my back. I'm not going to cry about any dumb shoes.
    But when I'm writing my spelling words later, every word
looks like the word *shoes*
and my grip is so tight
on my pencil I think
it might bust.

On Saturday Grandma says, "Let's check out those shoes you're wanting so much. I got a little bit of money set aside. Might be enough—you never know."

At the shoe store, Grandma turns those shoes over so she
can check the price. When she sees it, she sits down heavy.
"Maybe they wrote it down wrong," I say.
Grandma shakes her head.

Then I remember the thrift shops.

"What if there's a rich kid who outgrew his or got two pairs for Christmas and had to give one of them away?"

We ride the bus to the first thrift shop. Black cowboy boots, pink slippers, sandals, high heels—every kind of shoes except the ones I want.

We ride the bus to the second thrift shop. Not a pair of those shoes in sight.

Around the corner is the third thrift shop. . . . I see something in the window.

Black shoes with two white stripes. High-tops.

Perfect shape.

$2.50.

THOSE SHOES.

My heart is pounding hard as I take off my shoes and hitch up my baggy socks.

"How exciting!" Grandma says. "What size are they?"

I shove my foot into the first shoe, curling my toes to get my heel in. "I don't know, but I think they fit."

Grandma kneels on the floor and feels for my toes
at the end of the shoe.

"Oh, Jeremy . . ." she says. "I can't spend good money
on shoes that don't fit."

I pull the other shoe on and try to walk around.

"They're okay," I say, holding my breath and praying
that my toes will fall off right then and there.

But my toes don't fall off.

I buy them anyway with my own money, and I squeeze
them on and limp to the bus stop.

At home a few days later, Grandma puts a new pair of snow boots in my closet and doesn't say a word about my too-big feet shuffling around in my too-small shoes.

"Sometimes shoes stretch," I say. Grandma gives me a hug.

I check every day, but those shoes don't stretch.

I have to wear my Mr. Alfreys to school instead.

One day during Math, I glance at Antonio's shoes.

One of them is taped up, and his feet look smaller than mine.

After school, I head to the park to think.
Antonio is there—the only kid who didn't laugh
at my Mr. Alfrey shoes.

We shoot baskets—a loose piece
of tape on Antonio's shoe smacks
the concrete every time he jumps.
I think, *I'm not going to do it.*

We leap off the swings.
I'm not going to do it.

We race from one end of the playground to the other—
"I'm not going to do it!" I say.
"Do what?" Antonio says, breathing hard.

Grandma calls me for supper and invites Antonio over, too.
After supper, he spies my shoes.

"How come you don't wear them?" Antonio asks.

I shrug. My hands are sweaty—I can feel him wishing
those shoes were his.

That night, I am awake for a long time thinking about Antonio.
When morning comes, I try on my shoes one last time.

Before I can change my mind, the shoes are in my coat.
Snow is beginning to fall as I run across the street to Antonio's
apartment. I put the shoes in front of his door,

push the doorbell—and run.

At school, Antonio is smiling big in his brand-new shoes.
I feel happy when I look at his face and mad when I look
at my Mr. Alfrey shoes.

But later, when it's time for recess, something happens.
Everywhere, there is snow.

"Leave your shoes in the hall and change into your
boots," the teacher announces.

Leave your shoes in the hall. It's then I remember what
I have in my backpack. New boots. New black boots that
no kid has ever worn before.

Standing in line to go to recess,
Antonio leans forward
and says, "Thanks."

I smile and give him a nudge. . . .

"Let's race!"

Maribeth Boelts is a former preschool teacher and the author of many books for children. Jeremy's story was inspired by kids she has worked with as a school volunteer, mentor, and coach in her community. She says, "I have often been touched by the generosity I've witnessed in children and their willingness to share, even when it's tough to do so. These selfless acts have a way of shaping lives." Maribeth Boelts lives in Cedar Falls, Iowa, with her family.

Noah Z. Jones is the illustrator of *Not Norman: A Goldfish Story* by Kelly Bennett, *The Monster in the Backpack* by Lisa Moser, and The Bed and Biscuit series by Joan Carris. About *Those Shoes,* he says, "I know exactly how Jeremy feels in this book, wanting something so badly it becomes all-consuming. In my case it was a probably a new, crazy action figure with 'kung fu' grip." Noah Z. Jones lives in California with his family.